NORWOOD HOUSE  PRESS

Wasps, Hor[...] and Honeybees

By Kathleen Corrigan

Search for Sounds
Consonants:
h, w, y

Scan this code to access the Teacher's Notes for this series or visit
www.norwoodhousepress.com/decodables

DEAR CAREGIVER, *The Decodables* series contains books following a systematic, cumulative phonics scope and sequence aligned with the science of reading. Each book in the *Search for Sounds* series allows its reader to apply their phonemic awareness and phonics knowledge in engaging and relatable texts. The keywords within each text have been carefully selected to allow readers to identify pictures beginning with sounds and letters they have been explicitly taught.

When reading these books with your child, encourage them to isolate the beginning sound in the keywords, find the corresponding picture, and identify the letter that makes the beginning sound by pointing to the letter placed in the corner of each page. Rereading the texts multiple times will allow your child the opportunity to build their letter sound fluency, a skill necessary for decoding.

You can be confident you are providing your child with opportunities to build their foundational decoding abilities which will encourage their independence as they become lifelong readers.

Happy Reading!

Emily Nudds, M.S. Ed Literacy
Literacy Consultant

3

h

8

w h y

HOW TO USE THIS BOOK

Read this text with your child as they engage with each page. Then, read each keyword and ask them to isolate the beginning sound before finding the corresponding picture in the illustration. Encourage finding and pointing to the corresponding letter in the corner of the page. Additional reinforcement activities can be found in the Teacher's Notes.

Wasps, Hornets, and Honeybees
w

Pages 2 and 3	Insects live all around us. We see ants crawling on the ground. We feel mosquitoes creeping up our arms, looking for a tasty place to bite. We hear flies buzzing about the kitchen. And we often see wasps in many different places.
	Wasps live all around the world except where it is extremely cold. They don't live in water, but they are often near water so they can drink. Wasps can be found in the woods and open places. They can hide in grass, in the ground, or under porches and behind sheds.
	There are many kinds of wasps. Some are very big and some are teeny tiny. Because wasps are insects, they have six legs. Many of them have wings. Wasps also have a very skinny part in their body that is sometimes called their waist. Many years ago, some women wore special clothes so they could have a wasp waist, too!
	Wasps are not bees and they don't make honey, but they are very busy.

Keywords: waist, wasp, water, wings, woods

h

Pages 4 and 5

There are many kinds of wasps. Some wasps are called hornets. Hornet nests can be found in many places. Some are built hanging from the roof of a house. Some are built in house attics. Others are built in holes in the ground, or hollow trees and logs in the woods.

A hornet queen will start to build a nest. The nest looks like it is made of paper because it is made with chewed-up wood. Some nests are as big as a basketball! This will be the home for all her eggs and, later, for the grownup hornets. All hornets will protect their home, so people and animals should leave them alone.

Hornets can be good for people's gardens. They like to eat other insects which would eat the garden plants.

People are often afraid of hornets because they can sting you and it hurts. One hornet can sting you more than one time, too. So be careful.

Keywords: hamburger, hand, hat, head, hearts, holes, hornet, house, hurts

y

Pages 6 and 7

Yellowjackets are another common type of wasp. They like to eat sweet things, so they might bother you at a picnic or BBQ. They might come for your yogurt or soda or fruit.

Like all wasps, a yellowjacket queen lays eggs. Tiny yellowjacket eggs have yolk to feed the growing insects, but yellowjacket eggs do not look like a chicken egg and yolk!

Yellowjackets have sharp stingers. If you get stung by a yellowjacket, you will probably let out a big yell! Just try to stay away from them. Don't wave your hand at a yellowjacket. Doing so might scare it, causing it to sting you. Leave it alone and ask a grownup for help.

Keywords: yell, yellow, yellowjacket, yogurt, yolk

13

Read this text with your child as they engage with each page. Then, read each keyword and ask them to isolate the beginning sound before finding the corresponding picture in the illustration. Encourage finding and pointing to the corresponding letter in the corner of the page. Additional reinforcement activities can be found in the Teacher's Notes.

h

Pages 8 and 9	Honeybees might look a bit like yellowjackets and other wasps, but they are not wasps. Honeybees are hairy and wasps are not hairy. Honeybees have waists and wings, but honeybees are not as skinny as wasps. And honeybees don't come to BBQs or picnics!
	Honeybees live in a hive with many other honeybees. The queen is the boss of the hive. Worker honeybees get food, build honeycombs, and protect the hive. Sometimes they need to find a new home and a big swarm of honeybees will fly together to set up a new hive.
	Honeybees are very important. They pollinate flowers, fruits, and vegetables. When a honeybee leaves a flower, bits of pollen stick to her. Then, when she goes to the next flower, she leaves some pollen behind. The new pollen helps the second plant grow seeds and fruit. Butterflies and hummingbirds help pollinate plants, too.

Keywords: hairy, hedge, hive, honeybee, hummingbirds

w, h, y

Pages 10 and 11   Wasps can sometimes be pests, but we need honeybees. They are pollinators and they make the honey that we love to eat.

Bees like blue, purple, and yellow flowers. The flowers that the honeybees visit can make honey have different tastes and colors. Honey can be yellow, golden, orange, or even brown.

Beekeepers make hives for honeybees. The honeybees have safe, warm homes where they can make enough honey for the bees to eat, as well as some for the beekeeper to collect and sell.

Inside the hive, the bees make beeswax. The beeswax is used to make honeycombs. Honeycombs are rows of little hexagon-shaped pockets that can hold honey, pollen, and eggs.

The beekeeper makes sure the honeybees have enough honey for the winter. Then the extra honey is put in bottles and sold to people who want a yummy treat.

Keywords: hexagon, hive, honey, honeybees, honeycombs, wagon, wasps, wheels, white, yellow

Norwood House Press • www.norwoodhousepress.com
The Decodables ©2024 by Norwood House Press. All Rights Reserved.
Printed in the United States of America.
367N—082023

Library of Congress Cataloging-in-Publication Data has been filed and is available at
https://lccn.loc.gov/2023018612

Literacy Consultant: Emily Nudds, M.S.Ed Literacy
Editorial and Production Development and Management: Focus Strategic Communications
Inc. Editors: Christine Gaba, Christi Davis-Martell
Illustration Credit: Mindmax, Tranistics
Covers: Shutterstock, Macrovector

Hardcover ISBN: 978-1-68450-722-1   Paperback ISBN: 978-1-68404-864-9
eBook ISBN: 978-1-68404-923-3